For Harry and Mary Ellen,
who always brought rainbows into my life

SIMON & SCHUSTER BOOKS FOR YOUNG READERS
An imprint of Simon & Schuster Children's Publishing Division
1230 Avenue of the Americas, New York, New York 10020
Copyright © 2017 by Jessie Sima
All rights reserved, including the right of reproduction in whole or in part in any form.
SIMON & SCHUSTER BOOKS FOR YOUNG READERS is a trademark of Simon & Schuster, Inc.
For information about special discounts for bulk purchases, please contact Simon & Schuster
Special Sales at 1-866-506-1949 or business@simonandschuster.com.
The Simon & Schuster Speakers Bureau can bring authors to your live event.
For more information or to book an event, contact the Simon & Schuster Speakers
Bureau at 1-866-248-3049 or visit our website at www.simonspeakers.com.
Book design by Lizzy Bromley · The text for this book was set in ITC Lubalin Graph.
The illustrations for this book were rendered in Adobe Photoshop.
Manufactured in China · 0317 SCP
4 6 8 10 9 7 5 3
Library of Congress Cataloging-in-Publication Data
Names: Sima, Jessie, author. · Title: Not quite narwhal / Jessie Sima.
Description: First edition. · New York : Simon & Schuster Books for
Young Readers, [2017] · Summary: Born deep in the ocean,
Kelp is not like the other narwhals and one day, when he spies a
creature on land that looks like him, he learns why.
Identifiers: LCCN 2015041713 (print) · LCCN 2016020366 (eBook)
ISBN9781481469098 (hardcover : alk. paper) · ISBN 9781481469104 (eBook)
Subjects: · CYAC: Unicorns—Fiction. · Narwhal—Fiction. · Identity—Fiction.
Classification: LCC PZ7.1.S548 Not 2017 (print) · LCC PZ7.1.S548 (eBook)
DDC [E]—dc23 · LC record available at https://lccn.loc.gov/2015041713

Not Quite NARWHAL

JESSIE SIMA

Simon & Schuster Books for Young Readers

New York London Toronto Sydney New Delhi

Kelp was born deep in the ocean.

He knew early on that he was different from the other narwhals.

His tusk wasn't as long as everyone else's,

he had different tastes in food,

and he wasn't a very good swimmer.

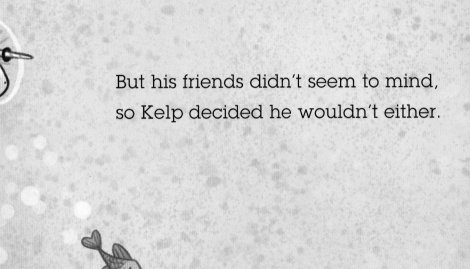

But his friends didn't seem to mind,
so Kelp decided he wouldn't either.

That is, until he was swept away by a strong current.

I wish I were a better swimmer!

Kelp found himself at the surface, closer to land
than he'd ever been before.

High up on a cliff he spotted a mysterious, sparkling creature.
It looked so familiar. It looked like . . . Kelp!

Kelp swam
toward land as
fast as he
could,

which wasn't
very fast
at all,

hoping that he
could catch up
with the creature
that looked just
like him.

When he finally reached the shore,
Kelp felt a little bit anxious—he had never left the ocean.

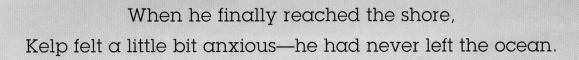

He was nervous about walking for the first time,
but the land creatures made it look so easy!

It wasn't.

Eventually he got the hang of it.

Everything on land was strange and beautiful—
but also kind of scary.

Kelp began to think
he might never find
the creature that looked
just like him. But as he
stumbled out of the forest . . .

LAND NARWHALS!

Kelp had never heard of unicorns before. They taught him all sorts of new things about his tusk,

they introduced him to unicorn delicacies,

and they showed him how to gallop.

There was no doubt that Kelp was, in fact, a unicorn.
He was having so much fun that he didn't want to leave.

But then he remembered all of his friends under the sea.

Kelp missed them terribly,
so he said good-bye to the unicorns
and returned to the ocean.

Come back soon!

Kelp swam
toward home as
fast as
he could,

which wasn't
very fast at all,

hoping that the
narwhals would still
like him now that he
was a unicorn.

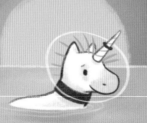

When he finally arrived, Kelp had butterflies in his stomach.

Kelp took a deep breath and told his friends the news.

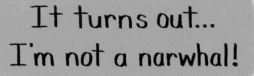

It turns out... I'm not a narwhal!

Of course you aren't.

Kelp was happy to be home, but now that he'd experienced life on land with the unicorns, he couldn't seem to forget them.

Did he want to be a land narwhal
with the unicorns . . .

or a sea unicorn with the narwhals?
Kelp couldn't decide.

But then he realized that maybe . . .

just maybe . . .

he didn't have to choose.